DOGTOWN SHUFFLE
A Short Story from the Geotek Universe
By J. La Grua

ISBN 979-8-9937851-1-0
First Edition

Published by ZeroPoint Publishing
An imprint of Little Lantern Creations, LLC
Printed in the United States of America

Cover design by J. La Grua

Dogtown smells like burnt fry oil, piss, and ozone—in that order. By noon, the alleys are thick with steam from wok fires and shorted power lines, the air greasy enough to slick your teeth. Late afternoon sunlight filters through the quietly flapping camouflage netting shading me from overhead.

I lean on my stall counter—really just a shipping pallet set on a couple of crates and covered by a musty surplus canvas tarp—stacked with CommPak shells, half-charged lithiums, and a cyber-arm I'm stripping for parts. A scrounger kid, named Shiv, eyes the arm like it might crawl into his backpack on its own.

"Not for *you*, runt," I say. "You want a limb, you pay *limb* prices."

He vanishes into the crowd. *Good riddance.* But he'll be back. Sticky fingers and all.

Little does he know there's more than this one limb. Stashed in my duffel next to it is a trove of goodies: I've got ultra-high-speed, Artificial General Intelligence, neural-net logic units with their serials lasered off; contraband batteries hot enough to power half a block; a couple of chips that still smell like fresh-off-the-die MilSpec. And the capper: eight matched pairs of tactical encryption/decryption modules matched with their key generators.

But this isn't for my normal clientele. Not by half. This is my *Special Reserve*—and it's earmarked for one of my heavy-hitter clients. It's not treasure, *exactly*, but in Dogtown, junk turns liquid if you know the right buyer. A month of meals fits in one duffel—with maybe even a little leftover—if you don't mind the weight.

The aisle breathes in jerks. In the next stall over, a woman with a prosthetic thumb haggles over a bottle of battery electrolyte like it's French perfume; a faulty servo makes the first joint twitch. Sniffing the cap, she swears it's cut with vinegar. A kid brandishes a cracked tablet like Baron Samedi waving a rosary-wrapped totem, swiping dead glass—going through the motions.

Across the way, the Gun-Runner stall is doing its usual brisk business. The clerk is armed with a ubiquitous, well-worn, *Avtomat Kalashnikova* AK-109. It hangs blithely on a quick-release sling, its stock folded, as he inspects the empty chamber of a matte-black machine pistol, before handing it across the counter to a couple of *obvious* narcos wearing *de rigueur* silver-capped, anaconda-skin cowboy boots.

Two stalls down, a man in a double-breasted suit coat and faded SpongeBob pajama bottoms sells SIM carriers from a velvet tray. Somebody grills soy-something-or-other on a warped hibachi; it smells like hope in teriyaki sauce. *Probably rat.* Turning back to the arm on my counter I adjust a servo with a jeweler's screwdriver, tweaking the force-feedback one notch at a time till the trace peaks on the oscilloscope flatten out to zero.

Suddenly, I see motion in my peripheral. I glance back up—The Runt, back skulking around my wares—eyes and nose peering above the edge of my counter.

Surprise, surprise.

I palm him a micro-fuse while I scold him for casing me—it's as if the drive towards thievery is implanted in the womb. In Dogtown, certainly nobody would argue against that. He glares at me like charity is poison and he melts back into the steam.

The magnifiers hum against my temples while I trace a solder bead along the cyber-arm's circuit spine. Heat haze blurs the micro-traces into a golden river. Somewhere off to my left, something shifts—a scrape, a breath.

"Goddammit *Shiv*, I told you to *beat it*—," I mutter, not

looking up solder flux hissing as the iron tip touches it, solder flows like water. "You're like a filthy little, kleptomaniacal boomerang... Well... you *break* it, you *buy* it—but you can't *afford* it. So I should say, you break it I'll be taking it out of *your ass*—"

Silence. Then a soft *clink*, the sound of a lighter lid. A rasp as striker wheel scrapes flint, the crackle of flint particles vaporizing as ferrocerium assaults wick at 3300°C. The faint sigh of flame.

I push up the magnifiers and blink through the heat shimmer as my eyes refocus. Not the Runt. Torch. He's crouched low beside the counter, lighter cupped in shaking hands, trying to coax a hit from a glass pipe so scorched it's more ash than glass. The flame catches, breathes, and he sucks hot air like it's salvation. Nothing burns. His pupils pinpricked; sweat beads on his temples. Classic AngelWire detox.

He exhales nothing and laughs—a dry, croaking wheeze that might've once been joy. "You know, Nix," he rasps, voice rough from a thousand scorched, empty pulls, "I got an angel on my shoulder... but it's also a devil. So heavy it makes me walk in circles."

I wipe my hands on a rag. "Well, if it's not my favorite, degenerate scumbag. Sounds like your theology's as busted as your lungs. Still sucking that glass dick, Torch?"

He grins a joyless grin through the tremor. "Still better company than you."

"Then maybe go preach somewhere else?"

Torch stands, flicking his lighter open and shut—a nervous

metronome. "Relax, *Docent*" he spits pejoratively. Heard you scored big. Thought maybe you'd want to spread the wealth?"

"Yeah, and I heard you were dead. At least I *hoped...*"

He shrugs. "Rumors of my demise... exaggerated. AngelWire's a hell of a resurrection agent." He leans in, flame twitching between us. "So what's the haul this time? More dead soldier tech? Maybe I can help you move it. Friendly discount. You gotta pay the Vig anyhow... House *always* takes a cut—"

In Dogtown, losers like Torch are a dime a dozen...

"Sure does, but *you* live on the *streets*."

A beat for emphasis.

"HARD pass."

  ...I'd like to kill the motherfucker who's supplying the dimes.

He picks up a half-stripped circuit board, holding the opposing corners by the tips of his index fingers, making it spin, absentmindedly, by flicking it with his middle finger; turning it over like a pinwheel relic. "You always *were* sentimental about your scrap."

Somewhere down the lane, a crash—metallic, loud, followed by a chorus of angry shouts. Everyone's heads swivel. Instinct says trouble. My gaze flicks toward the noise—just for a second.

When I turn back, Torch is all innocence and grins. "Guess that's *my* cue," he says. "I'll be seeing ya' around—Stay safe, Nix..."

He tosses the circuit board back onto the pile, carelessly, and slips away into the steam. He doesn't realize that just one of the chips on that board is worth more than his entire, sorry existence. I look down—bag flap crooked, zipper half-open. I pull the zip shut, scowling, chalking it up to paranoia. I toss the duffel under the counter.

Dogtown's full of hands. You never feel them until they are wrapped around your throat.

From a distance—faint at first, getting louder—the rhythm of a skateboard nearing. CLACK-CLACK... CLACK-CLACK. High-durometer wheels beat the gaps in the concrete like a loan shark owed money. 97As. I know that slap anywhere; everyone does. Kick's herald.

A skateboard knifes between two stalls, ollies a milk crate full of ancient frequency-hopping radios, and locks into a 50-50 on an I-beam anvil. Sparks spit.

"Uncle Nix!" she yells.

Transition to a wall-plant kickflip, clean landing. Then a textbook power slide that'd make Tommy Guerrero squeal. She comes to a stop; the vintage Powell-Peralta Rat Bones let out a long groan as polyurethane sands concrete. Hard as steel, faster than a purse-snatcher on crank. Blessed by Steve Caballero himself.

Kick deftly pops the board up into her hand without looking, with a nonchalance born of years of repetition. She leans the board against the counter pedestal and kneels down.

"Who's a good girl—you're the good girl." The German shepherd pup, Fluffy, flips to her back, demanding a belly rub; Kick obliges and plants a kiss on her head. "...MWAH!" Then she pops up in front of my counter, arms spread wide with an exaggerated, "HEY!"

She's quite the sight: ratty black hoodie covered in patches—so many patches I'd argue there's no original fabric left. Her hacked and amateurish undercut is a half-botched, half-schizophrenic dye job of clashing neon colors, like the 1980s barfed up a thrift store full of tie-dye. Her scarred, Kevlar kneepads tell a tale of a misspent youth as a street-hardened concrete warrior. I can sum her up in four words: Fourteen-going-on-bulletproof.

Kick raps the tail of her deck twice against the concrete—*tap-tap* —her street communion. Every run, every stunt. Like paying the street its due before she makes it bleed sparks. She's no blood of mine, this kid—street kids pick their own kin, and somewhere along the line I got picked for uncle duty. Better me than the gutter, I tell myself, though sometimes, I'm not sure the kid knows the difference. She's a handful, but all in all, it's not a bad gig.

"Morning, Uncle *Doom-and-Gloom*. I brought you *treasure!*" she chirps happily as she spins her battered and scuffed AR goggles around to the back of her neck, strap hanging down in front as she fishes around in her 1,000-denier courier bag.

"I'm working."

"You're *sulking*. Different sport." With an overdramatic flourish, Kick shouts, "TA-DA!! LUNCH!" as she produces a bruised, half-eaten apple that looks like somebody gnawed on it during a fistfight. "It's not *too* bad… if you squint at it…"

My stomach answers with a long, angry snarl — like a biker wrapping his throttle — loud enough to rattle the nearby aluminum shutters.

"I'm good," I lie.

Kick squints at me, clearly unconvinced. "Suit yourself,

Uncle Nix… but your guts disagree."

"It's called dignity."

"Pretty sure your dignity starved to death three days ago," she says, stuffing the apple back into her bag like she's saving it for my eventual surrender.

Kick continues digging around in her courier bag again. "OH! I almost forgot—" She produces a round, squat, plastic puck with a cracked face. "Signal scrambler!" she says proudly. "Kind of. I think. Found it in an old power shed under the causeway. There was a whole box of 'em, but this was the only one that wasn't soaking wet. Might be worth it if we can dry them out and clean up the boards—maybe they aren't too corroded?" She says it with the optimism of someone who has never *once* checked for corrosion.

"But if it's what I think it is, it makes drones barf all over themselves if you sweet-talk it right."

I tap the cracked casing. "Half-dead."

"Same," she says, and grins.

"But it's got one good cough left. Maybe even *two*. And besides, if it's half dead, that means…" she pauses for dramatic effect, then belts out, "IT'S HALF *ALIVE!*" She yells, drawing out the last word for emphasis, head thrown back, palms upturned making claw-like gestures. A maniacal cackle erupts from her wide-open mouth.

"MWAHAHAHAHAHA!!"

I blithely toss it under the counter, into the box labeled "Sacrificial Boards." Kick watches, pleased, grinning like a cat dropping a dead mouse on your pillow for you to find when you wake up.

"Sometimes, Kick? You're a *really* weird kid…"

"Well, you know… When The Going Gets Weird, The Weird Turn *PRO.*"

My CommPak buzzes:

—[DROP ETA TEN MIKES. STASH READY?]—

Client's "uptown." Too clean to walk these alleys, too paranoid to send a runner. The kind who pays triple so his loafers never touch Dogtown dirt. All he cares about is that the package shows up on time. All I care about is that he pays *cash*.

I thumb back:

—[READY ENOUGH. CASH ONLY.]—

Cash is king in Dogtown. Crypto's dead and Creds are a leash that ASTRA just loves to yank. Despite being outlawed across the WestPAC Annex, cash is still the filthy lucre of choice for every square inch of the Silicon Fold's dark underbelly. If you're going to use a lie that everyone agrees upon, at least it's one that Spéctarion's surveillance wankers can't track.

Kick is rocking back-and-forth on her heels, nodding toward my CommPak. "This the big score, eh? The one that gets us a view of the ocean and a toilet that flushes?"

"Don't get ahead of yourself. It's a month of meals, at best. If I don't screw it up. Besides, if you want a view of the ocean, you can always camp out down The Strand."

"Cool. I'll start picking curtains and throw pillows! So what is it?" she asks, her chin coming up, as if poking at the cyber-arm disassembled in front of me.

"Some kind of hot-shit neuro-mechanical arm—looks like it came off a bot, but this is no bot I've ever seen before." I gesture toward the arm with a jeweler's screwdriver. "I mean, just look at this!" I tap the screwdriver on the arm's chassis.

"...This thing's heavy-duty. Maybe even military. All I know is someone went to a lot of trouble to engineer this thing."

Overhead, a wheezing drone whines past, rotors hiccuping in uneven time. It dips low, banking left and right. Still makes me flinch. The real ones don't sound like that.

I duck behind the counter, stuffing the now-reassembled cyber-arm back into the duffel with the rest of the stash, zipper rasping like a file on steel. Moving through a blind inventory of the duffel's contents, my fingers stop mid-count.

Something's off.

There should be *eight* matched pairs of encryption modules— every set a Castor and Pollux of prime-number voodoo. But the last row in the foam cradle sits lopsided, missing its mate.

Seven and a half. Fuck.

The math burns. The light load means no sale. No payday, *no food.*

"That motherfucker!..." I growl. The image of Torch sucking hot air through that glass pipe flickers behind my eyes—his grin, the lighter clinking, the quick hands.

He grabbed one of the twins. Dumb move, fuckwit. You can't sell *half* a set; it's like fencing one *shoe.* But my buyer won't take seven and a half pairs *either.*

So now we're *both* broke, and I'm *still* on the hook.

I zip the duffel shut, jaw clenched tight. Dogtown's favorite equation: Nobody wins, everybody bleeds. Today it's Torch.

"Oi, Nix!"

Kettle's across the lane, hunched over her battery cart. Soldering iron clenched between yellowed teeth, solder smoke curling around her like incense. She waves with a shaky hand. "Whatcha got, Kettle?" I shout.

"You hear?" she calls, brushing aside shoulder-length dreadlocks wound with the alternating, color-coded guts of ancient Cat 8 cables. "…ASTRA sniffers on the causeway. Black wagons, heavy turrets. Sweeping south with a phalanx of FaceRec drones in tow."

My stomach tightens; the Argus Strategic Tactical Reconnaissance Authority—ASTRA—doesn't come here to get kittens out of trees…

"They're always sweeping *somewhere*," I say. "They're like cockroaches. In more ways than one…"
Kettle spits on the iron's tip; a loud hiss emanates as the gob of saliva evaporates—droplets of solder spatter onto her steel-capped boot. "Not like *this*. Four G-Wags. Full load. Like they're hunting."

Kick's eyes flick up. "That's not scrap rotor noise, is it?"

"Not yet," I tell her. Inside, I'm already mapping exits.

Kettle taps her iron on the cart frame—*tick-tick*—then holds it near my mask. "Hear that?" she says. "Actuator's whining half a kilohertz high. Drone mics pick it up when they hunt." She grins around the iron. "Not that you'll ever let them that close." I make a mental note to fix that later.

She was a grid tech once, before ASTRA folded the co-ops. Lost a brother in a sweep—wrong face at the wrong checkpoint, no appeal, just ash in a government urn. She keeps the urn under her batteries. Says it stabilizes the voltage. I pretend to believe her.

CommPak buzzes again—Torch.

—⟦I KNOW YOU"RE DOING A DROP TODAY. DON'T GET STUPID. YOU KNOW WHO TAKES A CUT.⟧—

I send him the digital middle finger:

—⟦ 凸(ಠ_ಠ)凸 ⟧—

"Go fuck your hat," I scoff in exasperation. I show Kick my CommPak.

Torch doesn't own me. But he clearly covets my *entire* stash of MilGrade encryptors. He doesn't even know about the rest of my stash. Thankfully, or he'd be lusting after a cut of that, *too*. Torch probably heard about them, or at least heard I was putting together some kind of deal. The problem is, he fucked himself by taking *one* of the modules, and by proxy, he fucked me—fucked my deal—nine ways from Sunday.

...And now I have to go deal with that sub-literate waste-of-a-sperm-cell and walking hair-clog.

Torch once lost to me in a big trade that he snoozed on—he passed on a loot crate he thought was junk, that it was a bad trade. Turns out it wasn't, and now he thinks every piece of shiny scrap that passes through Dogtown is owed to him as tribute. Typical Torch logic—if it's valuable, he deserves a cut—Just. Because.

Dogtown isn't feudal; it's feral. It has teeth...

And it's *rabid*.

Kick's mouth twists. "That mouth-breathing meathead still stealing my oxygen?"

"Pfft. Regrettably. "

"Lemme crack his shins." She gesticulates with her deck, holding it aloft by the front truck. "You know... 'For Instructional Purposes Only'."

"*Soon*," I say, chuckling. "He nicked my gear and now I'm gonna hang him by his ankles from a billboard and shake him till he gives up my shit, or gravity does it's evil, evil work—whichever comes first." I grin wryly. "Wanna tag along?"

"You betcha!" Kick exclaims "I'm always down to see Torch get his ass beat!"

I tuck the loaded duffel under the counter and scatter a pile of circuit cards from the dead-board-box onto my counter, just as the hum of the drone arrives.

Not junk. No squeal. The real thing—clean, surgical, the sound of money shaved into blades.
ASTRA drones, coming in hot and heavy.

Instinctively, everyone in the market flips up their hoodies and tucks their heads down. I yank down on my 'QR mask' and feel the actuators hum. It throws a shifting, undulating, 3D, black-and-white encoded lattice from across my face—creating angles where a face shouldn't have them—forcing their geometry solver to choke. The real trick is the "update." Hundreds of miniature actuators in the mask, combined with the alternating black and white voxels, reflect the LIDAR lasers back to the drones' sensors in such a way as to constitute a binary burst transmission.

This transmission, the GORGON subroutines, spoof a signed maintenance packet, in truth an obfuscated trojan, that the hive thinks it sent, and replicates throughout the drones' meshNET. The packet manifests nine seconds of fail-safe hover—effectively freezing the drones in place—while a rotating checksum that never terminates eats their brains and turns them to virtual stone. If the wind's right, it goes to eleven. Follow-on transmissions can cause myriad malfunctions and unpredictable behaviors.

As the drones swoop low, culling every face they can, Dogtown holds its breath.

The first of the Echelon Unit's up-armored G-Wagons punches through the market like a battering ram, scattering plastic sheeting and scrap metal. Three more grind in behind it, matte-black, turrets swiveling like hungry heads. People scream, half scatter, half freeze. 'Kalashnikov Guy' panic-fires his battered, century-old warhorse, blind, in the general direction of the convoy.

Bad choice.

Remote-operated minigun turrets belch their response with a disgusted cough of copper-jacketed, tungsten-carbide rounds— short, controlled, precise. The vendor's torso evaporates in a pink mist before his gun—and his disembodied head—hit the ground simultaneously.

And then *he* steps out.

Lieutenant Robert Vale.

As he closes the door, the ASTRA crest is visible, looming large on the matte-black door; its motto in bold, block letters: "Omnia

Videmus." (*"We see all."*)

Tall bastard, a 2070s dickhead with a 1970's porn-'stache; armor polished cleaner than a scalpel. Helmet held in one hand by the strap, the other idling on his sidearm—thumb flicking the retention clip: open-shut, open-shut. *Click. Snap. Click.* A tic. A duel he runs in his head on a loop—one he always wins.

Everyone's heard the stories. He was Beverlywood Security Annex Sheriff until he cold-cocked a drunk, NorGrumLockMart VP at a checkpoint. Should've been black-bagged; but he got exiled instead, mindlessly patrolling the dark corners of Dogtown because that's what Spéctarion does with talent that conspicuously —and very publicly—steps on its own crank.

Now he lurks the streets of corporate Siberia. Officially it was a "disciplinary transfer," but everyone knows it's *exile*. Attempted career suicide manifested as a 9-to-5-persistent-vegetative-state.

Vale plants himself squarely in the lane, scans the chaos with dead eyes, then mutters something too low to catch. The trooper nearest him smirks.

We all know the line:

"Fucking Dog-Shit Town."

He taps his comms, voice clipped, surgical. "Echelon Two, high sweep. Echelons Three and Four, grid east. Turrets suppress north and west. Push the rats where I can see them."

Drones leap into the air from the roof of the second G-Wagon, scalpels humming. Spotlights slice the alleyways; civilians scatter like spooked cattle; vendors yank tarps; panicked shots pop and die.

Kick slides beside me, breath fast. "We, uh... we should

relocate. Now."

I sling on the duffel, stuffing in the scrambler puck for good measure. "Follow me."

Down.

I lift the pallet up, trapdoor-style, and we drop into the narrow service slot behind the stall. The market's bones: cable runs, broken ducts, a trickle of grease-water. I clip the stash bag to my chest rig to stabilize it then crawl.

"Left at the split," Kick whispers. "That right-hand ladder goes up under Kwan's noodle stall—dead end if his shutters are down."

"They are," I say.

"He owes me a bowl," she mutters absentmindedly, then, "Nix…"

I hear it too: the turrets corralling the flow, the hum of drones adjusting in formation, the wheeze of a hydraulic compressor as a wagon pivots in place.

"This isn't a sweep," I say. "It's a hunt."

"For us?"

"For the *stash*. Which is *us*."

We pop up in a shadowed alcove behind a dead billboard. The market has dissolved into motion: stalls overturned, neon signs sputtering, smoke and steam mixing into a sour fog. Vale stands at the center, the eye of the storm, holster clip ticking like a metronome. *Click. Snap. Click.*

Kick points. "Who polishes boots before raiding a *slum*?"

"Sheriff cosplay," I say. "Helps him pretend this is law."

"Cool," she says. "I'll call him Sheriff Sh—"

"Don't."

She grins. "What? I wasn't gonna say Shit-for—"

"Kick."

"Fine. Sheriff 'Bob', then."

"That I endorse."

My CommPak buzzes again—client pinging. Not helpful. Not now.

Two choices: bolt and live, or sit on the stash and risk getting mulched.

My legs want to run. The urge visceral and deep. Survival is the only rule Dogtown ever taught me that stuck.

But my hand brushes the weight clipped to my vest. *A month of meals.* Maybe enough to buy air that doesn't stink like transformer oil; enough to let me go outside *not* protected by a Level IV SAPI plate. Faces flicker—Kwan's noodle kid with the burn-scarred fingers; the twins who wired stolen power and laughed when it shocked them. Sweeps took them all. I told myself it didn't matter. But it *did.*

"*Not* this time," I whisper.

I attempt to boot the QR mask, but as it does its init sweep—testing the 3D actuators—it bleats a warning and shuts down. *Fuck. Time for 'Plan B'...* I thumb a burst code and slave my CommPak to the puck nestled in my duffel bag; I piggyback its cough with a ghost signal from my CommPak. Suddenly, every drone in four blocks freezes for nine seconds, then jerks left. Jerks right. Holding motionless then they smell blood three alleys east.

The swarm forms up then tears off into the distance, like a swarm of very pissed-off hornets. Vale's head cocks. The clip snaps a little faster.

Kick's eyes light. "Was that—"

"Your toy had a cough left. Good call."

She tries to swallow the smile and fails. *"Obviously,"* she says, smirking.

"Now we move."

We cut across rooftops through a warren of welded catwalks and missing planks. Kick floats like a bird; I grind like a man with rent due. The drones to swing towards our phantom. Troopers pivot into a pincer to box the market's north end. Vale doesn't hurry. He just waits for the city to push us where he wants. The drones can't target-lock us, but every time we pop up, they clock-and-lock our positions, predictive algorithms stitching the likely intercept points. Vale knows the math as well as the streets.

This stretch runs east toward the old tramway, near the north edge of the Mercado. If Vale's herding us—and he is—that's where the jaws will close. The city's a maze, but every rat learns the same traps.

A drone skims low—too close. It's twigged but still dangerous. We're sky-lined up here.

We can't stay high—too many eyes up there, and Vale only

needs three pixels of my silhouette to make my day go terminal. I yank open an old access hatch tucked under a rusted maintenance gantry; Kick slips in first. We drop into a narrow crawl tunnel that runs parallel to the defunct tramway —one of Dogtown's forgotten arteries.

Kick slams the maintenance door and throws a valve handle that looks like set dressing from a post-apocalyptic sitcom. It groans, then locks with a shudder that feels permanent. "He can't route around this," she pants. "This whole sector was condemned. Algorithms don't know the shortcuts the rats do."

We move fast along the maintenance catwalk, ducking pipes and old fiber trunks until the tunnel dead-ends in a T. No cameras. No drones. No algorithmic breadcrumb trail.

We bail out the side hatch—boots hitting street-level—right as Torch oozes out of the shadows like the world's surliest birthday clown.

He steps out of a doorway, thick-set, shaking and sweaty, sleeveless armored vest carved with burned-in sigils, random pieces of Dogtown's detritus dangle from the chest rig's MOLLE straps. Eyes always bloodshot. He flips his lighter—open, shut, open, shut. *Clink. Clank.* Not just a habit: a junkie's rosary, each spark a prayer to an angel of fire.

He doesn't even look at it anymore—just keeps time with the twitch in his skull.

"Well," he says. "Look who's walking my *street.*"

Kick's voice goes sugar-sweet. "Hiya, Torchy..." she sing-songs. "Thought ASTRA slung your junky *ass* in jail. Or rehab. Or a trash compactor..." she snorts loudly at her own joke.

"...Gods know that the Body Vats wouldn't want *your* purulent, bloated corpse."

Torch cocks his head, a puzzled look on his face.

"It means 'pus-filled,' you ignorant shitbag." She laughs mockingly as the words tumble out of her.

He smiles without humor tilting his head side-to-side. "*Cute.* You got a pretty smart mouth for a homeless gutter rat—"

"*HOUSELESS*, Motherfucker!" She blurts angrily, moving forward, board lifting toward the sky, shock pads humming. I grab her reflexively by the back of her hoodie to keep her from escalating things further. Even in his current state, Torch was still dangerous.

His eyes cut to me. "You *got* something of *mine*, Nix." He flicks the lighter open and closed. Repeatedly. Reflexively.

"Nothing of yours exists," I say.

"That's adorable. Hand it over before the black wagons make confetti outta your insides."

A drone hum threads the air. Close. Kick shifts her weight, the skateboard's now fully-charged shock-pads whining insistently right at the threshold of hearing.

Torch steps closer. "*Last* chance."

I feel Kick coil beside me. She'll go for the legs if I give a look. It'll work *once*. Torch has two backups in the doorway; their shadows move wrong.

"Get ready," I tell her, low. "Left gutter. Move on three."

"And you?" she whispers.

"Insurance."

"Don't do anything noble," she says. "It looks weird on you."

"Three!" I shout, but Kick is already moving—her board snaps to pavement, wheels singing; as she rockets past Torch's knee she dick-punches him on her way past, before he can react, forcing him to double over, then shoulder-checking the second shadow into a stack of plastic crates. The third reaches, grabs air, eats concrete.

Torch, recovering slowly, lunges for me; I give him the rest of the move: pivot, palm to wrist, *twist*. The lighter clatters to the ground. He swings clumsy, his brain too addled by the AngelWire plowing through his brain, and I slide past, shove him hard into the doorway, pulling off a textbook bump-and-switch—slipping the scrambler puck into his vest while, in the same motion, lifting the stolen encryption module.

The puck bleats awake, announcing its position to every drone within ten klicks. The drones above us hiccup, pivot, then commit.

Half the swarm shaves down the lane, the swarm forms up, hungry for the screaming target fed from the puck in Torch's pocket.

He barely sees them before they open their little mouths and vomit 20-mm chunks of copper-jacketed tungsten-carbide hate.

And Torch finally gets what he always wanted—to matter.
Even if it was only to a malevolent, psychopathic drone swarm.

The Mercado giveth, the Mercado taketh away.

At least today, it's taking out the trash.

I don't look back. Neither does Kick. The streets of Dogtown are full of bad choices and appropriate consequences. He thought *everything* valuable in Dogtown was *his* by right.

Guess the swarm disagreed.

Glancing up as we run, she complains, "That was my *toy*."

"Consider it a donation towards Urban Beautification."

"Fine. But you owe me a doughnut—make that *two*."

"Put it on my tab."

"Your tab's a rumor."

I flick open Torch's lighter and slide the grind wheel against my filthy jeans, fire erupting from the wind-shrouded wick. I hold it at shoulder level admiring the flickering glow, then snap my wrist, the lid snapping shut with a satisfying *clank*.

"Here... you can have this. Spoils of war," I say, tossing the lighter to her.

"Nice!" Kick exclaims, catching it and then stuffing it into her right cargo pocket; the brass clinks as it strikes the galvanized steel skate tool, oblong and heavy.

We continue dodging through darkening alleyways, between torched cars, fallen chain-link, overflowing dumpsters.

Within three hundred meters of the drop site, we skid into a half-collapsed metro tunnel, breath ragged. The air tastes like rust and battery acid. A spotlight lances in. Dust explodes in the beam.

Vale steps through the glow behind us, calm as a surgeon scrubbing in. Troopers stack behind him, holding at the entrance and block the exit. This kill is personal.

He looks at Kick first. Those dead eyes flick down, calculate, discard. Then they find me. His hand rests on the sidearm. The retention clip pulses.

"Cornered," he says, voice steady. "Drop the pack."

Kick's whisper brushes my elbow. *"Don't say it."*

I smile and say it anyway. "Sure thing, *Bob.*"

The clip ticks faster. A tiny twitch at the corner of his mouth. Rage leaking into the calm. I've heard he once killed a trooper for less.

"You think that's *funny?*" he asks.

"You don't look like a Vale," I say. "Bob suits you."

His jaw clenches. Finger hovers on the draw. For a heartbeat, he's just a man who got demoted for punching the wrong mouth and hates being reminded.

He breathes once. Discipline wins—barely. *"Pack,"* he repeats.

Kick sighs. "Here we go."

I raise my hands. "Relax, Bob. No need to get twitchy. How about I buy you a coffee and a doughnut?"

The trooper nearest him coughs a laugh and smothers it. The clip ticks triple-time.

"You think you can mouth your way out of Dog—" He stops himself. "Out of this?"

"I think coffee's cheaper than *bullets,*" I say. "And rumor says Beverlywood cut your expense account."

The gun comes up. Fast. The sheriff just decided the duel is real.

Down.

I throw Kick left as the burst cracks. Neon ghosts on the wall explode into glass rain. We dive through a maintenance door, slam it behind us. Bullets chew the frame, chew cinderblocks, chew my nerves. My ears are singing a disapproving song.

We run blind through a dark intestine of tunnels, Kick leading, leg pumping as she propels her deck faster, counting turns under her breath like prayers. "Two *rights,* one *left,* ladder down—her kicktail slaps concrete as she ollies up and then falls in a parabolic arc, into the open maw of the dark stairwell. All four wheels slap the floor at once at the base of the stairs, with a high-durometer *CRACK!* She crouches down then grabs a rail, power-sliding into a short, open crawl way, "WATCH THE *HOLE!*—"

"WATCHING!," I shout, panting, and *still* almost fall into it.

We surface in a storage yard choked with dead billboards and cage wire. Drones buzz the sky like hornets; somewhere, a wagon idles, patient as a big cat. Kick skates loops around me while I scan for the next hole.

"Up," she says, pointing. A metal stair climbs the side of a warehouse into scaffolding that doesn't look like it wants to be helpful. "That'll put us on the old tramway. Bridge to the roofs. Easy."

"Your 'easy' is a hate crime," I say. But I go.

Halfway up, the world goes bright. A drone finds us; the beam hits like a slap.

Move.

"*GO!*," I shout, which is redundant because Kick is already a comet.

Turret fire laces the scaffolding. Shards sing past. The stair bucks under our feet. We hit the tramway—a thin concrete ribbon over a mouthful of alley—and sprint.

Drones ahead. Drones behind. Vale on the street below, tracking us with that dead lawman gaze. He doesn't shout. He doesn't have to. The city moves when he looks at it.

"Faster," Kick says.

"You're a child," I wheeze.

"Yeah," she says, "and I'm dragging you like a Little Red Wagon."

She flicks a switch on her board. The little shock-pads spit blue; her wheels spark and pop. She grabs my wrist and leans, towing me the way a speedboat tows a drowning man. It works long enough to get us to the roofline. We cut across gravel and skylights. The stash thumps my chest. My legs turn to rubber. The air tastes like copper.

"*Left*," Kick says. "Then across the sign. Trust me."

"I'm overdrawn on trust," I say. "And I've definitely got a fucks deficit." But I follow. The sign is a rusted shell with missing panels, spanning a gap to the next building. She runs it like a balance beam, board clacking, arms wide. I shuffle after, praying to gods I don't like.

"Relax, Unc! If you fall, I'll tell everyone you died *stylish*."

We make it. Barely. The sign groans its opinion about my life choices—loud, and not very optimistic.

Vale appears on the far end of the roof behind us, stepping up from a fire escape with infuriating calm. His troopers fan to either side; the drones pull back to clear his line of fire. Holster clip sings. His thumb works the holster like it's timekeeping for executions. Every tic a promise that someone's name just got added to his scripture.

Vale kneels, drags a gloved finger through the gravel. He doesn't look at us; he looks at the tiny furrow our feet cut across the tar, the small stones kicked wide at knee height. He adjusts a half-step left. The muzzle lines up with where we're going, not where we are.

"End of the line," he says.

Kick breathes, "Don't—"

"Easy there, Bob," I say. Hands up, palms out. "No need to get all trigger-happy. I still owe you that coffee and a doughnut. Remember?"

The clip chatter goes feral—like he's trying to drown me in it. For a second I see him, not the sheriff, not the officer, just a bitter man dumped in Dogtown for doing one wrong thing, to one wrong person, the absolute wrong way.

In his rage he jerks the trigger. His machine pistol barks its complaint in a rapid staccato of audible exclamation points.

Anger pulls the muzzle a hair right. The burst takes a chunk out of a rooftop vent as the rounds scream off into the dark—arcing off toward points unknown.

By the time the ricochets stop singing, Kick has me by the collar and we're gone—over the lip, down a service ladder, into the lungs of the building. Shots rake the parapet a beat behind us.

We tumble into a stairwell that smells like mold and dead pigeons. Kick breaks free of my pulling grip. Stops.

"Hold up—there's something I have to do."

"Are you shitting me?!"

Close behind the rapidly approaching footfalls clomping in the stairwell above. Gaining ground.

"Trust me, Uncle Frowny-Pants..." Kick turns quickly and sprints back up to the nearest landing.

"What the hell are you doing?!" I shout. Kick leans her head around the corner and shouts, "HEY FUCKFACE! RON JEREMY CALLED! HE WANTS HIS MUSTACHE BACK!" Kick howls with laughter as she turns and hops down the stairs, three steps at a time.

We keep moving until our legs burn; vision tunnels, the world narrows to heartbeat and noise.
We don't stop until the sky opens again.

Several blocks away now, our trail a labyrinthine meander of dead ends, false fronts, hidden doors and blind alleys. The rooftop is quiet, deserted except for us and the pigeons, cooing in the coop that overlooks the ocean. The city is loud, buzzing with life, people returning to their previous activities. Like nothing ever happened. Falling into a state of willful amnesia. It's the only way to survive the insanity of these streets.

From up here, Dogtown looks almost peaceful—smoke rising in lazy spirals; neon signs blinking fitfully, through the haze like dying stars. The G-Wagons prowl the wreckage below, turrets sweeping alleys. Drones limp through the air on glitchy rotors. Somewhere down there, Vale fidgets with his sidearm, clip snapping in a rhythm I can't unhear.

Kick flops down beside the rooftop access door, legs out, board across her lap. She lets out a loud, exhausted sigh, pulls her vape, sparks it, then takes a drag she hasn't earned.

"That," she says, coughing, "was stupid."

"You dragged me like a sled."

"Well, you're heavy."

"And, you're disobedient."

She shrugs, grinning sideways. "Oh, *you* know you *love* me, Uncle. And you'd *literally* be lost without me. Like, SERIOUSLY— you'd *still* be out there, running in circles, tryin not to get your ass shot off by ol' "Sheriff Bob". For someone who was *born* here, you sure have a *shit* sense of *direction...*" The last part is uttered, dripping with sarcasm, while she looks up at me from under her tilted brows, her blaze orange and electric blue bangs partially obscuring her eyes. And *I* love *you*. You're the *only* family I *got*, Unc."

I look at her—at the neon hair she butchers herself with stolen clippers, at the ratty hoodie and the sticker-bombed board and the eyes that have seen too much of this life but still want to see more of it despite it all. She's an orphan with a map of every dry corner in the South Bay burned into her brain, and a backpack full of junk she calls *treasures*. She sleeps on couches and in warehouses and under stairwells and still thinks curtains are something you get to pick out.

"Yeah," I say. "I love ya too, *kid*. My problem child." I put my arm around her and pull her into a firm side-hug. "You sure keep shit interesting, kiddo..."

She hands me the vape. "You called him Bob. Twice."

"He hates it."

"I *noticed*. You gonna keep doing that?"

"Well, I'm not done being alive."

She nods, solemn. "Good plan."

"And *you!* You said he has Ron Jeremy's mustache!"

"I *KNOW!* Sorta makes all those hours spent digging up retro-porn all the more worthwhile—"

Kick offers me her vape. I drag it, hold it in, then hand it back. She takes a pull too.

"—you really *are* a connoisseur of that stuff."

We both fall silent for a second, staring at each other. Then we simultaneously explode with howls of laughter. We collapse into hacking laughter, smoke pouring out of our noses.

Kick's still coughing when she jabs me with an elbow. "You shouldn't smoke that, Unc. These things'll *kill* you…"
I look at the vape—*her* vape—still glowing in her hand.

I pull the stash bag tighter. *It's still full.*

Miracles happen in Dogtown; they're just *messy.*

I thumb my CommPak:

```
—[YO! GOT SIDELINED—'BOB' WANTED TO TANGLE.
HAD 2 BEAT FEET. GOT DA GOODS. I'M @ DROP
POINT ЬAⅡ—
```

—⟦OMW. B THERE IN :10⟧—

Below us, Vale sits at an intersection and looks up at the skyline. Eyes scanning. Rage burning. Even from here I can hear the faint *click-snap-clicks* as his thumb worries the holster. He says something I can't hear and the troopers scatter to new positions. The man's a *machine*. A broken machine, but a machine *nonetheless*. Him and his rabble of jack-booted psychopaths will be back tomorrow. *Same shit… Different day.*

And I'll be bobbing and weaving—ducking and dodging. In this town, the shuffle *never* ends. Every day it's a new hustle. Another deal closer to that impossible prize.

But I'll keep chasing it. Because it's all I've got. That and this lunatic teenager here.

I take a drag from the vape.

"Bob…" I say to the night, long and drawn out, just for me.

I exhale hard as I reflect upon the day. The word tastes sweet.

Kick elbows me. "Strong finish, Shakespeare. Want me to carve that on your tombstone when Bob finally plugs you?"

"Coffee and a doughnut," I say. "Don't spend it all in one place." The words climb, smug and sharp, proud of the hit Bob doesn't even know he took.

She snorts, then pulls a chain from around her neck, producing another trinket—a little brass key, polished to a high sheen, from years of rubbing against her skin. "Payment," she says. "For services rendered. Opens a lock somewhere in the world. We just have to find it."

I take the key. It's warm from hanging around her neck. I don't throw this one away. It's junk. Or it's not. In Dogtown, a key can open a closet, a vault, the right door at the best time, or the wrong door at the worst time. I pocket it anyway.

But some doors aren't for opening in daylight.

Kick smirks. "Told you it had two coughs left."

I grunt. She's right. She usually is, which is the problem.

The buyer pings with a sunflower again, like he sells joy for a living.

—[6A. SAME BAG DANCE.]—

He always says it like it's a prayer. Kick eyes the alley mouth. "He brought a friend. Shadow, left window, two floors up."

The window shadow doesn't smoke, doesn't fidget. He just breathes with the alley. Kick lifts her chin an inch—she's clocked his reflection in a tilted TV screen nailed to a wall. "Left," she whispers—a direction and a warning at once.

The hive pauses—seven, eight, nine—still counting ghosts even when the drones are gone. Old habits die slow.

My CommPak buzzes:

—[YOU STILL HOLDING? I'VE DECIDED]—

Another interested client.

I delete the message.

Somewhere uptown, this guy will wake to a very expensive hole in his shopping list. *He'll live.* In Dogtown, missed opportunities are a kind of a regular occurrence.

You snooze. You lose.

"Tracking. We're fine for now."

That's a Tomorrow-Nix problem.

"Pickup's in four. We get to eat tonight. Want burgers?"

"BURGERS?" she says incredulously, "I know I'm just some half-educated street urchin, but one thing I do know is nobody's seen a cow in 45 years. And you can dress up a block of tofu with horns, a tail and a big honking bell, doesn't mean I'm gonna *eat* that nasty *shit*."

"That's fair." I laugh. Well, you think about it and decide. You have three minutes until the buyer gets here.

"I dunno... I could *murder* a bowl of noodles."

I nod approvingly.

We sit a minute longer, breathing like survivors, listening to the patrols continue their prowl. The skyline hums with bad decisions and second chances. Tomorrow, there'll be new clients, new and more interesting ways to die. New holes to crawl through.

But tonight we're on a roof, *not* in a gutter.
The stash is intact.
The kid is alive.
We're going to fall asleep with full bellies for the first time in days.

And the sheriff of Dogtown *missed*.

It'll do.